MOUSE'S
FIRST SPRING

LAUREN THOMPSON

ILLUSTRATED BY
BUKET ERDOGAN

SCHOLASTIC INC.

New York Toronto London Auckland Sydney
Mexico City New Delhi Hong Kong Buenos Aires

To Katie and Nicky—L. T.

To my dear sister Emnos,
for all our differences and your sweet friendship;
and to a dear friend, Linda,
for your wisdom and support.
Thank you—B. E.

ISBN-13: 978-0-545-09621-8
ISBN-10: 0-545-09621-9

12 11 10 9 8 7 6 5 4 3 2 1   8 9 10 11 12 13/0

Printed in the U.S.A.   40
This edition first printing, January 2008

Book design by Mark Siegel

One windy spring day,
Mouse and
Momma went
out to play!

There in the grass,
Mouse found something
glittery and flittery.
What can it be? wondered
Mouse.

"Look!" said Momma.
"A butterfly!"

Then *whoosh!* blew the wind, and *fluttery buttery* the butterfly flew away.

There under a leaf,
Mouse found something
slithery and slimy.

What can it be?
wondered
Mouse.

"Look!" said Momma.
"A snail!"

Then *whoosh!* blew the
wind, and
hidey insidey
the snail hid away.

There on a branch,
Mouse found something

feathery

and plump.

What can it be?
wondered Mouse.

"Look!" said Momma. "A bird!"

Then *whoosh!* blew the wind, and
dip   flip   flap
the bird darted away.

There by the pond,
Mouse found
something
green
and peeping.

What can it be?
wondered Mouse.

"Look!" said Momma.
"A frog!"

Then *whoosh!* blew the wind, and

splishy splash

the frog hopped

away.

There in the dirt,
Mouse found something
pink and wiggly.

What can it be?
wondered Mouse.

"Look!" said Momma. "A worm!"

Then *whoosh!* blew the wind, and

squiggly squeeze
the worm slid away.

There on a stem,
Mouse found
something
sweet and petally.

What can it be? wondered Mouse.
"Look!" said Momma.
"A flower!"

Then **whoosh!** blew the wind, and *rumply bumply* **Mouse** tumbled away!

Then all
around, Mouse
felt something
soft and cuddly,
and oh-so-cozy.

What can it be?
wondered Mouse.

Smooch!
came a kiss

and *oooch!*
came a hug!

"It's me!" said Momma.

"Spring is here, little Mouse,
and I love you!"